His Fantasies,

Her Ecstasies,

This Is Our ReaLity!!

Aquilas Ville

Published in the United States of America

ISBN 978-1-955243-46-9 (SC)
ISBN 978-1-955243-47-6 (Ebook)

Aquilas Ville
222 West 6th Street
Suite 400, San Pedro, CA, 90731
quilville@gmail.com

Order Information and Rights Permission:

Quantity sales. Special discounts might be available on quantity purchases by corporations, associations, and others. For details, contact the publisher at the address above.

For Book Rights Adaptation and other Rights Permission. Call us at toll-free 1-888-945-8513 or send us an email at admin@stellarliterary.com.

Contents

Taste Test

ome days are good; other days are amazing. I'm a big fan of enjoying life and living it to the fullest. Who am I? My name is Romeo, and I am a sales manager at one of the biggest retail stores in the U.S. here in Atlanta. When it comes to women, I always had a knack for hooking up with the wildest. I am honestly proud of myself and even the women that I've met along the way that showed me everyone is different and special in their own way. Case in point: one time I came home from visiting my homeboy that was in town for the weekend. The first thing that came to mind as soon as I walked through the door was to lie down and get some much needed rest. I tossed the keys on the counter and headed for the bedroom. "Well well!! What do we have here" I said as I walked into the room and saw Kim, my lover of seven years, lying underneath the sheets. To my surprise though, another woman's head poked out of the sheets as both her and Kim smiled and giggled. It did occur to me that my girl found other women attractive. However, I never thought that she would actually get down with one. Nevertheless me being the man that I am, I walked over to the bed and jumped in between my girl and her friend Sasha, a bisexual woman that she met a few months back in December at a Christmas party in downtown Atlanta. I guess I was late because they were already naked. Sasha and my girl both leaned over and began tongue wrestling each other while I grabbed the both of their breasts and made my way down to their pussy lips. Sasha and my girl pushed me down and began yanking at my shorts. Kim pulled my dick out as Sasha leaned down and licked my dick head. Kim then kissed me on my navel then made a trail with her tongue all the way down to my dick and proceeded to suck and lick my nuts as well. Kissing my dick and sucking it like a lollipop, Kim took the dick out of her mouth and slapped it against her cheeks then smacked Sasha on the lips with it and slid it slowly inside her mouth. I told Kim to lie down and for Sasha to hover over her face. The two of them got into position as Kim held onto Sasha's thighs and begin to French kiss her pussy. I spread Kim's legs open and wiggled my lips against her clit, then tickled her pussy lips with my tongue and stuck my index finger inside her pussy to taste her honey. I leaned over to the nightstand and grabbed a Magnum condom out of the drawer and ripped it open, holding my dick steady with one hand while unrolling the rubber down on it with the other hand. Kim moaned as she let her tongue whirl around in Sasha's pussy, causing Sasha to grab her hair and close her eyes while rocking back and forth on Kim's face vivaciously. Sasha's legs trembled as she lowered her head towards Kim and made out with her. Loving what I saw, my dick made its way inside of Kim's vagina while I slap Sasha on the ass. Out of nowhere Sasha's phone rung. Kim failed to inform me that Sasha was married, because now she hopped herself up off of Kim and began getting dressed. Shaking my head. Sasha bent down and kissed Kim on the lips then waved at me as she made her way out of the door and downstairs towards the parking lot. Both Kim and I sighed. Just our luck.

The Outside Looking In

ome people just don't get it. It seems as though minding your own business these days is the hardest thing in the world to do. You would think that keeping up with your own life is hard enough as it is, let alone worrying about somebody else's as well. Apparently the Johnsons definitely did not get that memo. Nicknamed "MNC (Misery Needs Company), the Johnsons, an elderly couple who had been living on Stalum road for twenty years in the D.C. area were known for being the complainers of the neighborhood. If someone was complaining about something twelve times out of ten it was them. Ebony and Steven Williams, a married couple who moved into the neighborhood five years ago, had their fair share of run-ins with the Johnsons. Majority of the neighbors kept to themselves and rarely came outside, but a coin couldn't drop on grass without Sheila or Maurice Johnson poking their big head asses out of them old ass blinds in the living room or upstairs in their bedroom. Ebony and Steven did not mind though. Born from nudist families, both Steven and Ebony were comfortable being naked and enjoyed having sexual adventures anywhere at any time. On Mondays, which was deemed game night, they would have friends over for either poker or dominoes or spades or whatever else game that came to mind. One particular Monday night however, Ebony had an idea. She decided to spice things up a bit. Suggesting the game "TRUTH OR DARE" to everyone in the house, all of their friends and of course Steven agreed to participate. Truth answers floated around the room. However, none of Steven or Ebony's friends dared to pick DARE due to the fact they knew that they were going to end up in a situation in which they had to do something outrageous. Steven finally decided to pick DARE after being asked by Courtney, Ebony's friend since high school. "Steven, I dare you to have sex with Ebony outside on the sidewalk in front of everybody" Courtney said with the biggest grin on her face. Steven and Ebony smiled. They both got up from the couch and headed towards the front door. Courtney and her husband Aaron as well as Donovan (Aaron's brother) and his girlfriend Stacy followed behind, cheering them on as if they were walking through a hallway and headed out onto a playing field for the championship game. Steven grabbed a blanket from the hallway closet then bolted to the front door with such excitement. In his mind, this was just another escapade in the making. Being that it was 7pm and the sun had set, everyone pulled out their camera and put it record mode. Courtney grabbed the bed sheet from Steven and laid it across the sidewalk in front of the house. Steven walked over to Ebony and kissed her on the lips, lifting her up and laying her down on the sheets. Because Ebony was wearing a sundress and no panties underneath, sliding her dress off was a show in itself as everyone got to see her naked body instantaneously. Steven knelt down in front of Ebony and kissed her inner thighs as he unbuckled his belt while taking off his t-shirt simultaneously. "Hmph" and "damn" belched out from the crew as they were witnessing a real live porno in the making. Steven happily licked and sucked on Ebony's clit then stuck his tongue inside of her pussy, massaging her titties while Ebony latched onto Steven's afro and began to moan loudly. Donovan "adjusted" his pants as Stacy smiled at him because she knew what was on his mind. Ebony decided that she would return the favor to her wonderful husband. Signaling Steven to stand up, Ebony knelt down in front of Steven and licked his dick head then slid his mammoth dick inside her warm mouth, soaking it with her saliva as a trail of it leaked down Steven's cock and onto the sheets. She ran her fingernails up and down the side of his body, pushing her head closer to his dick while Steven grabbed her by the hair and forcefully slammed his cock down her throat. Cars driving down the street honked, some even slowing down in astonishment and sheer amazement at how bold Ebony and Steven were and the spectacle that was being put on for the world to see. Nevertheless, the nudist couple carried on like it was a regular day in the workhorse. Rock hard and ready to go, Steven told Ebony to bend over. He squatted over as she put her ass in the air and shoulders on the sheets, exposing her pink mango pussy in the process. Courtney and Aaron hugged each other with cameras in hand recording and smiling in the process as Steven slid his dick inside of Ebony's vagina. Adjusting her body to his size, Ebony looked back at Steven and moaned as she slowly rocked her ass back and forth on his dick with a smooth rhythm. Stacy leaned in closer with the camera in Ebony's face as Ebony smiled and swatted at the phone glaring in her face as Aaron got behind Stacy and made as though he was humping her from the back. "Smack", "smack", "smack" "that's right" "take this dick" as the sound of Steven's right palm made contact with Ebony's ass cheeks while he talked that sex talk to Ebony. "Yes daddy" "take this pussy" "beat this pussy" "you love this pussy" Ebony blurted back out, as she threw her ass back on Steven with force while he held her by the waist and catapulted his dick inside her wet pussy. While Donovan was surveying the street to see if any cops were coming, Courtney happened to look in the direction of the Johnsons and saw Maurice on the phone pointing at them. He called the cops. Damn. Courtney yelled out "cops" as everyone took off running towards the front door. Both Ebony and Steven got up and hurriedly put on their clothes then folded the sheets in a ball as they sprinted towards the door as well. The cop pulled up just as Steven entered his house. Steven walked back outside to the driveway as Officer Mosley got out of the squad car. Being that he knew what the officer was going to talk about, Steven explained to the officer that it was not what the neighbor made it seem to be. With a sarcastic look on his face, officer Mosley gave Steven a warning and told him to keep whatever shenanigans they were up to behind closed doors and in the house. "Thank you officer", Steven exclaimed as Officer Mosley got back in his car and pulled out of the driveway shaking his head while pointing at Steven and driving away. Ebony, who was standing in the doorway, watching the whole ordeal, looked at Steven. With the same thought in mind, Ebony and Steven both looked at Mr. Johnson and stuck their middle fingers up at him then waltzed back into the house.

World Premiere

"Monica, Monica, Monica", Anthony repeated as he talked to his friend Jeff on the phone while standing on the balcony of the penthouse in North Miami Beach that overlooked the beach and city streets. Reminiscing about their high school days and the adventures they were a part of, Anthony asked Jeff "did you ever hook up with Monica's friend Brittany from our biology class that was on the cheerleading team?" "I sure did. As a matter of fact, she called me yesterday". "That's wuz up" Anthony exclaimed as he took the hungry man meal out of the microwave and sat on the couch. "Jeff, Did I ever tell you the story of what happened with me and Monica one night when we went to the movies?" "You will now" Jeff said as he got comfortable and sat up on the bed lowering the volume on his TV and closing the room door so no one else in the house could hear what was about to be discussed. "Remember I told you that Monica was one of those girls that was a little on the wild side because she had a strict childhood and did not taste freedom until her senior year of high school?" "Yeah yeah" said Jeff. "Ok. One day you didn't come to school because you were sick or something like that. Monica and I were in class discussing how boring class was and how we rather watch paint dry than to listen to Mrs. Shatner's monotone voice all day. She told me about how she couldn't wait to go off to college and get away from her parents due to the fact that they were always up her ass and never gave her space unless she was going to the movies with her friends". "Hold on. My mom on the line", Jeff said as he clicked over." "Aight go ahead and continue Anthony", said Jeff. "Yeah so I asked her what was the last movie that she saw, and she said some crazy ass name I don't even remember. Nevertheless, I asked her would she like to go to the movies with me on Friday. In my mind, I was hoping that she said yes. Fortunately, she did. She also said that she was going to invite some of her friends as well. I already put it in my head that I was going to make a move on her while we would be watching the movies. I been wanted her sexy ass, so I said to myself that it's either all or nothing. "I feel you bruh. It be like that sometimes", Jeff said as he chuckled. "So boom Friday came around and I had just got out of school. I went straight to the barbershop by my house right after to get fresh. My barber hooked me up of course, so I walked out that shop feeling priceless. A few hours later, I got ready and grabbed Eric's car keys from the kitchen table and left. Eric didn't mind though. He knew his younger brother was sliding out with a pretty little baby because I brought her to the house before while he also had a chick over. As I approached Monica's crib, her older sister Nicki and her friend Diamond was in the parking lot waiting on her to come out. "Hi ladies", I said as I pulled up behind their car and turn off the ignition. "Wuz going on Anthony? You better be nice to my sister or imma beat you up", Nicki said as her and Diamond laughed. "Don't worry, I will" smiling as I got out of the car and walked around to open the car door for Monica. Monica and I waved at Nicki and Diamond as I backed out of the driveway and peeled off into the night. "Jeff bruh, you should've seen how good she was looking that night. I wanted to pull over so bad and eat her up right in the car, but I controlled myself. Lawd knows her perfume and them thick ass thighs showing from that skirt had my mind going and going and going. What made it even worse was that she was taking selfie pictures, poking her lips and taking pictures of her body. I almost ran in the back of a car paying attention to her fine ass. "HA" Jeff screamed. "I'm for real. Throughout the ride, Monica told me that her friends bailed out on her at the last minute for tonight. I pretended like I was sad about the shit, knowing damn well I was happy as I don't know what. We pulled up to the theatre and hopped out, speed walking to the door because the line was packed. After grabbing our tickets and a bucket of popcorn as well as some mountain drinks, we made our way into theatre 13. Since all of the seats in the back were filled and most of the middle seats were also filled, we made our way to the front row and sat down. As we both sat down, I caught a peep of her panties. I was ready. Her thighs were so damn thicccccccccck! As the movies started and the lights dim down, I "accidentally" spilled some popcorn on her. "Accidentally huh" Jeff said sarcastically. "Jeff you already know. I said sorry and picked up the popcorn crumbs from between her legs. On the way down, I slid my hands on her thighs. Monica looked at me and said "you know damn well what you was doing, ol nasty ass". I acted like I had no idea what she talking about. We both sat back and smiled. I leaned over and whispered in her ear "what's on your mind?" "Nothing", she said as she pushed my face away and told me to stay on my side. "Playing hard to get huh" said Jeff. "You already know. It's all good though. All men know that when a woman says one thing, twelve times out of ten she really means something else. I complimented her on how she looked and smell. She said thanks. We made small talk throughout the movie and even cuddled up a little. At this point, I felt like I had to take a leap of faith and get more physical. I kissed her on her neck then whispered in her ear "would I be wrong if I told you that I would give it to you right here and right now in front of all these people?" She laughed and looked at me wide eyed. I was so serious and she knew that. Here's the interesting part though Jeff. She looked at me and said "would you look at me differently if I told you a secret?" "Not at all", I said as I rubbed on her thighs and kissed her on the lips. "I always had a desire to fuck in the movie theatres. Don't judge me, but that's just how I feel". "Nawwwww" Jeff exclaimed. "Yeah. I was shocked my damn self. I told her that I understood how she felt and that I definitely wasn't going to look at her funny or think anything of it because I want to do the same thing. She smiled. Jackpot. Because the mood was set, I decided to get a little mannish. I slid my hand underneath and pressed my hand against her pussy. Monica looked at me with that "it's about to go down" look. I moved her panties to the side and slid my middle finger in her pussy while kissing her lips. She put her purse on the empty chair next to her then adjusted her skirt up, making it convenient for my hand to maneuver down there. The couple that was sitting next to me peeped over and watched as Monica stood up then kneel down in front of me. I unbuckled my pants and pulled my dick out as Monica grabbed it and circled my dick head with her tongue. Putting my hands behind my head and sitting up, I watched as Monica spit on my dick and jacked it a little before sticking it in her mouth and suck it good and I mean good. "Damn bruh I should've been there", Jeff said. "Bruh, even though I was the one that started it, I still couldn't believe that it was actually going down. Live and in primetime too. After a few minutes of sucking me up I tapped Monica on the head as I stood up, dick hanging and all in front of everybody. By this time, almost half of the people in the theatre's attention had shifted from the movie to Monica and I. Monica looked around and smiled, then pulled down her skirt as I sat down and signaled her to come sit on top of me and ride this dick just how I like it. She grabbed my dick and held it up as I put the Magnum condom on. Slowly, she turned around with her ass facing me and squatted down on my log while grabbing my ankles. I watched her ass move up and down in my lap while I slapped both ass cheeks continuously. The rows behind us cheered us on as we put on a show. We decided to switch positions as I stood up and bent her over, raising her right leg up and putting it on the armrest. I stuck my dick inside of her pussy and began pounding away. She moaned and moaned "um hmmm" "um hmmm" "hell yeah" "get this pussy" as I threw my dick inside of her then pulled it out and did it again several times. Our bodies rocked back and forth as I wiped the sweat off of my face and waved to the crowd, while a barrage of flashes from cameras blinded me. After several minutes of that, I slapped Monica on the ass as I laid down on the floor. She positioned herself on top of me with those lovely red pump heels still on her feet. Those pumps made it a piece of cake for her to maintain her balance as she grabbed my dick once more and slid down on it. Almost instantly, her pussy latched onto my dick as she put her hands on her hips and started popping her ass on my dick and twirling her body around. I was surprised security didn't bust in there and throw our asses out. Spreading Monica's ass cheeks open so she could feel this entire dick inside of her, she began beating my dick up with her fat ass. That was letting me know she was about to cum something serious. With that in mind, I lifted up my waist and slung my dick inside of Monica while sucking on her pretty ass titties and massaging them as well. With all of her might, Monica let out a loud ass moan "oooooooooooo shit" as her body contracted violently and she fell over onto my chest. Cum leaked out of her pussy like crazy and all over my thighs then onto the ground as people in the theatres clapped and cheered wildly, some even giving us napkins to wipe our face. We both laid there for a few seconds, body to body breathing heavily and thinking about what just happened. Damn I miss her. She was one of a kind, ya feel me Jeff? Hello? Hello? Helloooo?? Jeff fell asleep on the phone. "Talk about a motion picture", Anthony giggled to himself as he hung up the phone.

You Feel Me???

ow this pussy feeling right now, any man that catches my eye could and would get this box something serious and I mean instantly. I hate being up late at night, bored out my mind and horny as hell. Going to the club would probably make this pressure I'm feeling worse. All that grinding and throwing my ass back on some random dude would've been nothing but trouble for him. This pussy can make any man put a ring on it the same night because I would've unleashed the beast on his ass. Men are so lucky they do not have to deal with the shit us women do. My ex-boyfriend Marcus could tell you. Whenever we fucked, he would look at me like I was possessed. I used to suck and fuck him so good that some days he would call out of work due to the fact that he did not have the energy to step foot inside that construction site, let alone operate machinery. Just like most men though, Marcus could not keep his dick in his pants. You would think that after loving him, treating him like royalty, pussy and head whenever and wherever he wanted it that he would at least have the decency to be honest with me and tell me that he was sleeping around with other women. Shaking my head. I guess that's how love goes. YOU win some, YOU lose some. These lonely days and horny nights aren't making life any better either. I don't understand how some women do it. Go months or years without sex??? SHIDDDDD!!! More power to y'all. Just thinking about the way Marcus would moan my name "Jazzi (short for Jasmine) whenever he came makes my pussy lips moist. The feeling of his elephant dick growing while inside of me and massaging my pussy walls and how he sucked on my breasts and bite on my neck then suck on my bottom lip is driving me crazy. Why me?? Why the hell did I have to be the one laying here in this big ass bed, pillow between my legs and thinking about sex instead of being on top of his dick getting nut after nut?? When I broke up with Marcus, it was devastating not only because he cheated but the fact that I found a man with a hurricane tongue and a horse dick. I be hearing that stupid ass statement "size doesn't matter. It's all about the motion in the ocean". Let them tell it. They sure as hell wasn't talking to me. I need and love me a handsome, big dick man. The head is just a bonus. His head does not have to be all that, just as long as he knows how to maneuver inside this pussy and leave me dicknotized. I'm short (only 5'4), so I love being on top riding that big ass dick and watching my ass jiggle on it, or when I'm lying down on my stomach with my ass tooted up in the air pushing it back on the dick and feel it hardened up in my pussy. When I tell U I be feeling all of that dick!! Humph!! The best part is when a man takes my long hair (thanks to my Jamaican mom and American dad) and wraps it around his hand then grabs me by the back of my neck or in the front by my throat and rams that dick inside of me. Shit!! I need to fan myself. There aren't too many men out there fully equipped. It's usually great dick or great head and that's that shit I don't like. Having a tongue prance around in my pussy then moonwalk down my ass crack will have me cross-eyed and cumming like crazy. A man knows when he has me. My legs feel like rubber after sex. Going to the bathroom becomes a mission if the sex is the bomb because I get so damn weak. I also love how a man's tongue parts my pussy lips open like the entrance sliding doors to a retail store and have me foaming like a bubble bath. If it feels too good, imma try and push his head away but my weak ass knows I am not overpowering no man. I just lay there and wait until he's done or until dick is hard enough for him to remove his face from my pussy. Riding a man's face and how he holds my thighs in place while gripping my ass cheeks at the same time and having me seeing stars and shit. I must admit that at first I was scared of anal. I thought I was going to die the first time I tried it. My suggestion ladies: if you want to try anal then get you a man with a little dick. They don't have much to work with anyways, so with a little lube you'll be taking it in the ass in no time. My freaky brave heart ass mistakenly tried it with Marcus big dick ass once. My goodness! I was sore as hell for a few days after that episode. When I finally got use to it though, it was all systems go with Marcus and I on that note. I made sure to bounce that ass on his dick every time we did anal. I had him cumming in no time. I totally understand why women love that raw dick shooting cum inside of them though. It feels like an arrow being shot through water. My tubes are tied, so Marcus loved cumming inside of me. I could feel his nut running down my thighs and legs right now. Pardon me. Those flashbacks be everything. DAMN YOU, BIG DICK!! I do enjoy how the dick feels when it's about to cum though. A ten inch feels like a twelve inch, particularly when those veins come out of nowhere and resemble thick ropes wrapped around the dick. Cum go to pouring out the dick be looking like a volcano erupted. It be funny though when a man cums. If men knew how ugly they looked when they cum, they would look away instead of being all up in a bitch face looking like they broke a bone or something. In my mind, I be laughing my ass off at them. I don't want to bruise their ego so I keep those thoughts to myself or my home girls and I get a good laugh out of it. I can't blame them though. Pussy is amazing. Hell I even tried pussy myself a few times, so I can imagine how a guy feels. All this talk about sex got my pussy wet as fuck. I would call my home girls, but they're probably getting their back blown out right about now or fast asleep. Lucky bitches. That's my girls though. We were meant to be friends. I have no problem having sex in front of them and vice versa. We all grown. I would love to be cuddled up or even in a sexual position right now. Oh well. It is what it is. Let me take my horny ass back to sleep.

The Sound Of Love

"How he hell did you and Chris manage to do that without getting caught by the janitor or somebody?? Y'all two some brave hearts. Not me. I don't care how horny or drunk I am. That's some off the wall shit there", Isabelle said as her and Carla laughed and gossiped while sitting on the couch, drinking and carrying on into the wee hours of the night. Carla and Chris, her boyfriend of four years, was the adventurous outgoing dynamic duo which made them perfect for each other. Granted Chris was nonchalant and more laid back, having only a few friends who resided in New Jersey. However, Carla was his best friend. Being that Houston has always been such a big city and so much to do here, Carla and Chris were inseparable. She loved his boldness and bravado, and he loved her feistiness and classy yet freaky personality. Carla was the type of friend regardless of what the plan was, she was down with you. Her sweet compassionate side though is what really attracted Chris to her. Carla was a voluptuous woman who carried her weight very well, and she had a sense of humor out of this world. She did not mind being the first person on the dance floor at any social gathering, which is how she met Chris who was a local DJ at the time. Isabelle little sister, Christina, graduated from college with a Bachelor's degree in Information Technology. Isabelle and Carla met each other at a clinic in which they worked in different departments. Isabelle was a billing code specialist, while Carla was the receptionist at the front desk. Both of them had a common enemy: a woman named Maria, who was the supervisor. Maria was a woman in which everyone had to see things her way. As far as she was concerned, no one could tell her anything. The day the scandal broke out all over the clinic that Maria got caught with one of the Janitors inside the female bathroom for a so-called "quickie" was the happiest days of Isabelle and Carla's life. Maria was fired the next day. Majority of the employees, including Carla and Isabelle went out and celebrated that same weekend as a matter of fact. "Wait till I tell Erica about this. She's going to blow your phone up like crazy. Let me call her right now", Isabelle said as she laughed and called Erica. "Erica! Let me tell youuuuuu! Carla right next to me and girl she got a story to tell. "Carla, tell her what happened Saturday night at the station". "Damn girl just give the story away then shit", Carla said as she snatched the phone away from Isabelle. "As your cousin was saying, Chris and I did something out of the ordinary Saturday while he was at work at the radio station. "Ooooo shit I want details, and you better not skip over any details", Erica exclaimed as she sat on her couch in the bedroom. "Ok. Here it is. Saturday afternoon Chris went to work as usual. He told me that he would be working late and for me to not wait up for him. I was like ok, but in my mind I was like hmmm. I already made my decision to surprise him at the station. It was 11:00pm when I got to the station. Because I knew the password to the building, I took the elevator to the seventh floor then the stairs to the eighth floor. It would've been too obvious if I just came walking out of the elevator, which was right in front of the radio station. They had two entrances; one in the front and one off to the side. I slid in the side door and crept up behind Chris and put my arms around him as he sat at his desk, listening to the caller's give their various opinions about artists and reality shows. He damn near flipped me over before realizing that it was me by my hands and the perfume I had on. Turning around, he said "baby what you doing here"? "I wanted to surprise you because I missed you. Sounds like you don't want me here" I said as I hit him with the sad puppy face. He smiled and said "now you know that's not true. I was just shocked that you would come here this late". "Then y'all did it", Erica said. "No girl not yet. He pulled me close to him as I sat on his lap. His dick was hard as fuck. I'm talking about I felt it through my tights. Chris was on air, so he told the viewers that he was going on commercial break. He took off the headset and set it down on the desk. He kissed me then kissed me on the neck, which y'all already know is my spot. He massaged my breasts then ran his hands up my thighs as I felt my pussy slowly turn into a pond. I got up from his lap and started to dance in front of him seductively. I moved my hips from side to side then turned around and bent over and shook my ass in his face. He was ready. As I was bent over, I felt something warm and thick brush up against my tights and my pussy. Chris turned me around and bent me over on the desk. I had no idea when he took off all his clothes, but he was butt ass naked in the station! "Damn girl like that?" Erica said as her and Isabelle both listened attentively. "Yep just like that. Let me finish let me finish. So all of a sudden, I felt his dick slide up my ass crack. I shivered like I was in a freezer from that shit. Chris pulled down my tights and put his dick right in my ass slowly, expanding it and making my pussy wetter than ever. I moaned so damn loud that he took his right hand and put it over my mouth. As I moaned and lunged forward from the impact of his dick rocking back forth inside of my pussy, I accidentally hit the "ON AIR" button. We both saw the light come on, but neither one of us cared or even made an attempt at this point to turn it off. The dick was feeling too good, and I know this pussy had him in ecstasy. Chris took his hand off of my mouth and crossed my arms together behind my back then slapped me on the ass as he continued bulldozing his dick inside my ass. My pussy was foaming and juices was all over the desk because I was cumming like crazy. I guess the thrill of thousands and maybe even millions of people listening to us fuck turned me on so much. Had anyone would've walked by that room, all they would have heard was skin slapping and curse words followed by a desk rocking. After a few minutes, Chris unhanded me then sat on the desk as I dropped to my knees and started eating his dick up like a candy bar. I got nasty with it too. I drowned that dick in spit then slurped on his balls and put it right back in my mouth as I held onto the desk for leverage. He was moving his legs around and all you could hear was "damn you sucking this dick" "that's right. Eat that dick up" as my head bobbled back and forth with saliva oozing down my chin and onto my breasts. Chris then stood up and told me to lie down on my back. He stood over me in the opposite direction with his ass facing towards me as he dipped his dick down in my pussy. I ran my fingers up his ass crack then then stuck my middle finger in it gently and stroked it a little then removed my finger and proceeded to squeeze his ass as he fucked me with so much rage. When I tell you I loved every minute of it. "Wow. So he let you play in his ass? Damn I want a man like that" Isabelle said as her and Erica chuckled. "Yes girl. Chris don't care about that. We was in the moment. I looked towards the desk and could see the lights blinking like crazy. Dozens of people were calling in, trying to figure out what was going "ON AIR". Chris got off of me and started jacking his dick, letting me know that he was about to cum. You know my freaky ass hurried and got on my knees right in front of him in attention, ready for daddy. I closed my eyes and felt his warm cum splatter on my nose and forehead. Some of it did get in my hair, which I hate because I had to go home and wash it out. "Aha ha ha ha ha whew help me" Erica laughed as her and Isabella could not control themselves. "That shit is not funny. I kissed Chris on his dick and licked the rest of his cum that leaked out and let it sit on the tip of my tongue as he looked at me, smiling and shaking his head. He knew he had a freak bitch on his side. Grabbing a napkin off of the desk, Chris wrapped it around his dick. He normally does that because even minutes after he cums, some of it still will spill out. I ran to the bathroom with my purse that got all my stuff I needed. We got dressed as Chris grab the mic and got on air trying to sound all sexy and said "this is the sound of love signing off. Goodnight and sleep tight". He shut the power off and locked all the doors then closed the station as we both made our way into the hallway and onto the elevator. "I am not going to lie. That story made me horny as fuck. I want some dick now" Isabelle exclaimed as Erica agreed and said "OK". "That shit was off the chain. Chris and I went home, showered up and took our asses straight to bed right after. The next morning, he called me while he was at the gym saying that his manager just called him. The manager fussed at first because of what he heard while he and his wife sat at home listening to the radio show. He did say however that the stunt we pulled skyrocketed their ratings and that he was proud of him. Chris told me he laughed and said "thank you sir" as his manager said no problem and hung up. I guess it worked out for everybody. "I bet you were scared Chris was going to lose his job or something" Erica said. "I was, but when he told me the rest of the story and his station was killing the other late night stations in the Houston area because of our little session, I felt like I helped him accomplished something monumental. "Girl shut yo ass up. Tryna sound all heroic and shit" Isabelle said as they all laughed.

About the Author

Goofy and nonchalant yet charming, Aquilas takes you inside the world of various singles and couples who not only walk on the "WILD SIDE": THEY LIVE THERE!! Aquilas has a passion for not only the sexual side of things, but also the intimate side as well. Like most people, Aquilas knows that there is more to a person than meets the eye.